The Revenge of the Substitute Teacher

The Revenge of the Substitute Teacher

Jan Lawrence

AN
APPLE
PAPERBACK

SCHOLASTIC INC.
New York Toronto London Auckland Sydney

ISBN 0-590-05902-5

12 11 10 9 8 7 6 5 4 3 2 1   8 9/9 0 1/0 2/0

Printed in the U.S.A.   40

First Scholastic printing, January 1998

For my mother, Claire, and
my father, Jim, with love.

Contents

1.
It's August 31st. Do You Know Who Your Teacher Is?

By the end of the fourth grade, everyone knew that there were two things you never wanted to happen to you in the fifth grade. First, you never wanted to get Mr. Manlin for a teacher. Second, you never wanted to land in the same class as Larry Hensack.

Mr. Manlin had a reputation for being the strictest, meanest teacher in the whole fifth grade. No, make that the strictest, meanest teacher in the whole school. As for Larry, let's just say his mother should have warned the world and named him *The Terror*.

Three years ago, my older brother, Dillon, had Mr. Manlin for his fifth-grade teacher. He'd been trying to scare me and my friends all summer. Dillon said if we got Mr. Manlin, we could kiss our life good-bye.

My dad actually requested Mr. Manlin for Dillon. Dad thought that Manlin was just what Dillon needed. My brother had gotten into a little trouble at school the year before. I have to admit, he did seem to clean up his act. In fact, he was so nice it started to get annoying after a while.

Anyway, back to me. I hardly ever got into trouble, at least not with teachers. So I didn't think I needed to learn any big lessons. In fact, my dad said if I kept up the good work this year he might consider getting me the dirt bike I wanted.

Believe me, I planned to try my hardest this year, even if it required studying. I just hoped it wouldn't be with Mr. Manlin. Every day I checked the mailbox to see if anything had come from the school.

My friend Matt and I called each other every day to see if the other one had heard anything. Matt said if it didn't come soon, he was going to call the school. I hoped I wouldn't have a nervous breakdown in the meantime.

When the phone rang, I knew it was Matt. It was time for our daily check-in.

"Hey, Jeff, telephone," Dillon called from downstairs.

"Who is it?" I yelled back.

"It's the President of the United States. He said it's urgent."

"Very funny." I picked up the phone in the hallway. "I've got it. You can hang up now. Hello?"

"Hey. It's Matt. Did you hear?" he said, sounding anxious.

"I didn't check the mailbox yet. It came today?" My heart was racing. "Hold on."

I ran downstairs and blasted through the front door. When I opened the mailbox there was a big pile of junk mail and lots of bills. Then I saw it, addressed to the Parents of Jeffrey C. Malloy. The return address was "Springer Elementary." My hands were shaking wildly. I managed to rip it open. And there it was, my fate spelled out in black and white. I let out a scream that was probably heard all the way to China.

Jeffrey C. Malloy. 5th grade. Mr. Manlin. Room 512.

I ran back inside and picked up the phone. "I'm dead."

"Mr. Manlin?"

"What am I going to do?"

"You mean, what are *we* going to do."

"You got him, too?" I asked, trying to sound like I wished he didn't.

"Like the plague," Matt said.

I must admit, I felt relieved. At least if I had a good buddy in the class, I might have a chance at surviving fifth grade.

"Did you talk to anyone else?" I asked.

"Nope," he said, his voice sort of shaky. "I called you first. I was going to call Chris next."

"Horrible. This is horrible." That was all I could think of to say.

"Hey, maybe your mom has some pull with the

principal. I mean, she's always doing all that volunteering and everything. Why don't you ask her? While she's at it, maybe she could mention me, too. Think about it. I'll call Chris now and then I'll call you back."

I sat by the phone in a state of shock. From what I'd heard, Mr. Manlin believed that fifth-graders needed lots of discipline, and lots of homework. Supposedly this prepares you for middle school. I get enough of that discipline at home. *Why me?* I thought.

My brother came barreling up the stairs, took one look at me, and said, "Bye-bye. It's been nice knowing you." He must have overheard me screaming my head off at the mailbox. Then he laughed, pointed to the door, and told me he needed the phone and some privacy. That meant he was going to call Cindy.

I clutched the phone to my chest. "Not now, Dillon! I'm waiting for Matt to call me back. I want to find out who else got Manlin."

My brother didn't respond except to rip the phone out of my hands and yell, "Beat it, brat."

Dillon yapped on the phone for more than twenty minutes. As soon as he hung up, the phone rang. It was Matt again.

"What did you find out?" I asked.

"Chris got Manlin, too. Kyle got Mrs. Smith."

"Boy, did he luck out," I said, feeling envious and angry. Mrs. Smith was the one everyone

4

hoped they'd get. She still believed in the candy principle. The candy principle means she rewards good behavior with candy bars and gum. Sometimes she even brings in doughnuts, and at Christmas she made everyone these really awesome handmade presents.

"We need a plan," I said.

"Yeah? What?" he said, sounding defeated.

"Pizza's here," my dad called. "Wash up, guys." Pizza usually meant my mom was working late.

"I've got to go. I'll call you tomorrow," I told Matt.

I wondered who else would be in my class. Maybe my friend Jax had lucked out and got Mrs. Smith. Jax was in my class last year. I really liked her, mostly because she was the only girl who was even halfway nice to me. Once she started being nice, all her friends started being nicer, too. I was almost popular.

It was not like I was a geek or anything last year, but I *was* pretty skinny and I did have a lot of trouble getting my hair to look right. I'm cursed with the Malloy hair, thick and wavy brown. My mom bought me some new hair gel, so it was more under control. I'd had a major growth spurt over the summer, and I hoped I'd finally be as tall as some of the girls.

I had a feeling that even my improved looks couldn't save me. I could hardly sleep that night. The next morning, I called up Matt and Chris and told them to meet me at our tree fort at noon. The fort's in the woods behind my backyard. My brother must have been eavesdropping, because as soon as we got to the tree fort, Dillon and his goofy friend Weasel showed up. The tree house barely fits the three of us, so my brother came in but Weasel just stood at the top of the ladder.

"What's up, dweebs?" Dillon asked, jerking Matt's baseball cap over his eyes.

"Nothing much," Matt shot back in an edgy voice.

Weasel kind of squeezed his eyebrows together as if he couldn't believe what he just heard. "I wouldn't say getting Sergeant Manlin for the next nine months is 'nothing much.' Do you have *any* idea what you're in for?"

We didn't respond. He shrugged his shoulders and said, "Okay, I just wanted to warn you guys, because there's a couple of things you should know before school starts." He started going down the ladder as if he was leaving.

Matt called him back. "What things are you talking about?"

"Don't scare them, Weez," Dillon said, smiling. "Hey, maybe the guy has mellowed since that incident when that kid forgot to bring in his science project."

My brother patted Chris on the back. "Don't worry, guys. I'm pretty sure they've got laws against teachers doing that kind of stuff today. At

6

least, I hope so. Anyway, I'm sure Manlin has a fun side, too."

"Oh yeah, he's a real fun guy," Weasel said.

"Manlin's notorious for giving out impossible homework assignments on Halloween night. Usually he'll tell you to make a whole world atlas just to cut into your candy collection time," Dillon said.

Weasel made a pained face. "The morning inspections are the real killers. He walks from desk to desk and checks to see that everything is shipshape. Your nails must be immaculate. Your shoelaces must be even on both sides. If you don't pass, he'll make you hit the floor and give him fifty."

"I think you guys are just trying to scare us," I said.

Dillon shook his head. "You'll see. He's even got his own dress code. Sloppiness is one of the worst offenses you could commit. The creases on his shirts and pants are so sharp you could get a paper cut if you accidentally brushed against him in the hallway."

"Another thing," Weasel added, yanking the hair on the back of my head, "you might want to think about something along the lines of a buzz haircut. We could give you all a shave right now if you want us to," he said, trying to torture us.

I pushed his hand away. There was no way I was cutting off my hair that took me all summer

7

to grow out. I was starting to like the way I looked. "I'm not cutting it no matter what," I said, and I meant it.

"Well," Weasel said, "I'm just telling you he doesn't go for what he calls that 'unmade bed' look."

I looked over at Matt with his messy, curly brown hair hanging down on his freckled face, and his blue jeans with the holes in the knees. Then I looked at Chris, who looked like he'd been lost in the woods for three days. I thought, *We don't have a chance.*

"Well, guys, we're just telling you this stuff because we don't want you to go in unprepared," Dillon said. "Your only hope is if he gets sick a lot this year and you get plenty of substitutes. You're going to need the relief, believe me." He nodded for emphasis.

"Unless you get that nut case. What was her name, Weez?"

"Oh, that one. Ms. Wilder. We only had her for one day, but how could you forget her name? Man, that woman wasn't flying with both engines." Then Dillon and Weasel let out a wicked laugh and took off, kicking up a trail of dust with their bikes.

We all took deep breaths.

"Do you think they were lying? You know, maybe just trying to scare us?" Chris asked me, looking like he was about to cry.

"I don't know. It's hard to tell with Dillon and it's even harder to tell with The Weez," I said. "I was only in second grade when Dillon had Mr. Manlin, so I don't remember it very well."

"Did anyone hear who Larry Hensack got?" Chris asked.

"Yeah, I checked with Kyle. He said Larry got Mrs. Smith, too," Matt said.

"Yes!" I screamed. "At least I won't have to worry about him stealing the desserts out of my lunch box every day."

"Or being Krazy-Glued to your chair," Matt added.

"Or finding a piece of moldy broccoli inside your desk," I laughed.

"Well, let's look at the bright side," Chris said. "At least we're all in this together. For all we know, Mr. Manlin could turn out to be a decent guy."

We all nodded in agreement, but not one of us believed it for a second.

2.
Sergeant Manlin

It was the first day of school. But when I got out of bed, there was no sign of my usual first-day-of-school excitement. What I felt was more like dread. My dad lectured me at breakfast, talking about how I had to learn to get along with all types of people. I had already planned my strategy: Keep a low profile and do my work.

Trouble was, I wasn't in my seat for five minutes before the plan started to dissolve faster than an ice cube on a hot summer day.

When I first walked into my classroom, a lot of people were screaming, "Yo, Jeff," so I sort of felt like we were all in this together. As I was looking for my desk, I caught a scary sight out of the corner of my eye: Mr. Manlin. I was trying to get a good look at him, hoping that maybe he had eased up over the summer.

Unfortunately, he had a buzz cut just like Dillon said. Dillon calls it the "Camp Lagoon special." Mr. Manlin was probably about my dad's age. He was wearing pants that looked stiffer than my aunt Mo's meat loaf, and a mean-looking scowl on his face.

The bell rang sharply at 9:00. Mr. Manlin immediately stood up and shut the door. He slowly ran his eyes over the room. I think he wanted to assess what he would be dealing with this year. "Good morning, ladies and gentlemen. Welcome to the fifth grade. As most of you may already know, my name is Mr. Manlin and I'll be your Commander-in-Chief from now until June. As far as I'm concerned, my number-one job is to prepare you for life's next stage — middle school. If any of you have older sisters or brothers, you know that middle school is no day at the beach."

Then it happened. Right in the middle of Mr. Manlin's speech, I felt a slight sting on the back of my head. It had to be a spitball. I turned around to see what was going on, and there, to my horror, sat Kevin, one of the evil Boyez twins. That could only mean one thing: His brother, Eric, couldn't be far away. Sometimes Eric could be an okay guy, but Kevin was a bully. I threw him a dirty look and quickly turned back around in my seat. I turned my full attention back to Mr. Manlin.

"Now, you might be wondering what I expect of you," Mr. Manlin barked. "What I expect is a can-do attitude." He turned around and wrote "can do" on the chalkboard.

Mr. Manlin turned back around to the class and

continued to talk. "There will be no excuses, no bad attitudes, and absolutely no troublemakers. I want all of you to learn to follow orders. Can you do that, Mr. Boyez?" His eyes zeroed in on Kevin.

"No can do," Kevin spat back.

"Excuse me?"

I was holding my breath, afraid of what might happen next. I mean, everyone is on their best behavior the first day of school! At least until after lunch.

Mr. Manlin's face was the color of a hot red pepper. His eyes got all squinty.

"Mr. Boyez," he said, jabbing a finger at Kevin, "before I started teaching you little squirts, I spent ten years as a sergeant in the army. Over the years I had to deal with all kinds — punks, heroes, troublemakers, leaders, you name it. I snapped every last one of them in line. In fact, a few turned out to be some of the best soldiers our army had ever known. Some of them had the IQ of a radish, but they became leaders. Why? Because they had courage."

I saw Kevin slink down into his seat like a slimy, scared little worm. Mr. Manlin was still going strong.

"You might be asking yourself how one gets courage. Courage begins with self-discipline. The way I see it, you can be a cow, or you can be a leader. You ever watch a cow, Mr. Boyez? They just follow the other cows, never knowing where they're headed. But a leader, there's someone who knows where he's going. Today I'm looking for a few good leaders who will head up this class and show the cows the way. Do I have any volunteers?"

None of us cows responded. An eternity seemed to go by. Then I saw Mr. Manlin point to a hand that went up in the back of the class. I turned around. It was Jax. She looked exactly the same as last year. She still had her long dark hair, giant brown eyes, and a really pretty smile.

"Please stand and state your name."

"My name is Jacqueline Ray, sir, but everyone calls me Jax."

"Okay, Jacqueline Ray, you are assigned to roll call. Every morning I expect you to stand at the front of the class, call out everyone's full name, take the attendance record to the office, and, when needed, give out homework assignments. If any of you think you'll have any trouble taking orders from Ms. Ray, I'd like to know right now."

The class was silent.

"Good. Okay, next I need a Chief Inspector."

Everyone looked down at their desks pretending to be fascinated with their pencils so he couldn't make eye contact.

"Hmm . . . Ms. Ray, looks like this herd is going to need some work. I guess you'll have to select someone," Mr. Manlin suggested.

I looked up for a split second, and accidentally caught Jax's eye. I was done for.

"I select Jeffrey Malloy."

My heart crashed to my feet. I couldn't believe it.

"Mr. Malloy, please stand. Mr. Malloy, a messy desk is the sign of a messy mind. We can't afford messy minds in this classroom. Understand?"

"Yes, sir," I answered as fast as I could.

"Your job as Chief Inspector is to check all the desks every Friday to make sure they are in tip-top condition. I expect you to dump any desk that does not live up to my standards of neatness and organization. And there will be no food in this classroom with the exception of lunches. They are to be kept in your cubbies. Got it?"

"Yes, sir," I quickly answered.

"I also put you in charge of making sure that all of your classmates adhere to the dress code when we line up after recess. That means shirttails must be tucked in. No weirdo hairdos. No nose rings or other pierced body parts. I operate on a behavior demerit system. Five demerits results in one grade drop."

"Yes, sir," I said. *Great,* I thought, *I'm going to be the most unpopular kid in the class.*

He gave out a few more corny assignments. One person was our Line Monitor, which meant whenever we had to line up the person had to check the line, making sure the kids were quiet.

15

Someone else was the Homework Collections Officer. Chris got the job of Paper Distribution Chief, which meant he was the paper-passer-outer.

Manlin wasn't finished yet. "Now that we've got our leaders lined up, I'll fill you in on a few more things. I'm sure you're all wondering how I feel about homework, right?"

A couple of people answered, "Right."

"Well," he continued, "just like all of you, I hate it. I hate to plan it, and I hate to give it."

I breathed a sigh of relief. Finally, there was something good about Mr. Manlin.

"I absolutely detest it," he continued, "which is why I give it each and every night, each and every holiday. Hard work is just one stop on the road to good self-discipline."

I had a feeling this was going to be one long year.

"Remember this," he warned. "We must all be on constant guard for the enemy that can bring us to our knees. Who is that enemy? Laziness."

By the end of the first week he had us all repeating goofy character-building sayings like "A chain is only as strong as its weakest link" and "There's no such thing as a good excuse." I quickly realized that a year with Mr. Manlin wouldn't be as bad as I had originally thought. It would be far worse.

3.
Double Trouble

Just when I thought things had hit rock bottom, Larry Hensack was transferred into our class during the second week of school. Mrs. Smith couldn't handle him. The rumor was that Mr. Manlin said he was looking forward to having the infamous Mr. Hensack as one of his pupils.

Larry came stomping into class, totally disrupting everything. He looked like a minigangster. His hair was all slicked back except for one piece that hung in his eyes, and he had a nasty expression on his face.

Mr. Manlin stopped teaching and looked at him. "Welcome to my classroom, Mr. Hensack," he said calmly. "I've saved you a special seat right next to my desk."

"You mean welcome to my nightmare," Larry muttered under his breath.

Mr. Manlin didn't miss a beat. He just kept talking about what he expected of us. Then, out of nowhere, he walked over to Larry and shouted, "Hit the floor and give me sixty. There will be no back talk in my class, Mr. Hensack. Do I make myself clear?"

I wondered why it took so long to come up with that. Maybe Mr. Manlin operated on some sort of electronic delay.

Larry reluctantly hit the floor. As he struggled with each push-up, I could actually see the reflection of his face in Mr. Manlin's highly polished shoes.

Mr. Manlin looked at the class and said, "You see, I heard Mr. Hensack's rude remark when he walked into my classroom. But, if you took note, I didn't react immediately. Why? Self-discipline. If I had reacted immediately, I might have given him a hundred."

I glanced at the kids on either side of me. I doubt any of us had ever met a guy like Mr. Manlin.

At recess, a bunch of us were shooting baskets. Jax and her friend Becca came over and asked if they could join us. Before I could even open my mouth, Jax grabbed the ball from my hands, slam-dunked it, and threw it back to me. "Practiced over the summer. What do you guys think?"

"Show-off," I said. But I was impressed. I was about to slam-dunk one myself when Larry came strutting over with his bebop walk and told us that Mr. Manlin was going to be really sorry for what he'd done. Apparently, his mother's brother, "Uncle Butch," was going to have a talk with Mr. Manlin about what he had done to Larry.

"You were acting like a jerk, Larry," Jax said, giving him a disgusted look.

Larry shot for a basket but missed, then said, "Yeah, well, I can *guarantee* I'll get a little more respect after my uncle Butch has a little chat with him."

We all just looked at him. What was he talking about? Larry could see he had everyone's attention, so he started smoothing down his greasy hair with a comb and trying to act really tough.

"Just wait," Larry threatened. "Uncle Butch will set him straight."

According to Larry, his mother's brother rode a Harley and had muscles like cinderblocks. Supposedly he was an ex-boxer and could knock you out just by breathing on you.

"I wish I had an uncle Butch," Matt said. "My parents think Mr. Manlin is the best thing to happen to me since my Super Nintendo broke."

After recess, we forgot about what Larry told us, because we were too busy just trying to transform ourselves into rocket scientists who could keep up with Mr. Manlin's surprise brain drills — as he called them. Everyone was sweating bullets. Winging it in Mr. Manlin's class was going to be impossible. He had built-in radar for you if you weren't paying attention. I have to say, Mr. Manlin definitely had the class under control.

By Friday, it was time for me to do desk inspections. I hoped everyone would pass. I decided ahead of time that unless someone's desk was a total pigsty, I'd let it go. I breezed down the aisles. Then I came to Larry's desk. Before I could even crouch down to look inside, I could detect a sickening odor coming from his desk. I stalled for a minute to consider my options.

Of course, I could do my job and dump it. If I did, though, I was a goner. But if I let it go and maybe said something to Larry in private, sooner or later Mr. Manlin would smell it and I'd be blasted for dereliction of duty. Well, after a few seconds I decided I'd rather deal with Mr. Manlin.

So I bent down and looked inside Larry's desk, holding my breath, pretending to really be giving it the once-over. Larry and I locked eyes, and he had this "in your face" smirk like he was daring me to say a word.

"Looks good to me," I said convincingly while I threw Larry a dirty look. Everybody in the class passed desk inspection, except for Julie. Her desk looked like our kitchen junk drawer, and I couldn't just let everyone go or Mr. Manlin would get suspicious. So I dumped it and she started to cry. Mr. Manlin sent her to the nurse. Boy, did I feel like a jerk.

"Nice," I heard Jax say sarcastically under her breath. A couple of the other girls looked at me like I was a mass murderer or something. I could see my newfound popularity going downhill faster than a sled on an icy hill.

"Okay," Mr. Manlin announced when I was finished. "I'd like to think that this will be the one and only dumping of the year." He looked right at me. "But that would only be wishful thinking."

Then he charged over to where Larry was sitting, looked inside his desk, and dumped. Stuff was rolling everywhere: dried-up grapes, a piece of old pizza crust, orange peels, and a few things I couldn't identify. One looked like half a Sloppy Joe from Tuesday's Wild Boar cafeteria special.

My heart jerked to a halt. Mr. Manlin walked over to my desk and said sternly, "You don't become a leader by winning popularity contests, Mr. Malloy. You both get three demerits and instead of going to recess on Monday, you'll both be making our classroom a cleaner place. I will bring in a few old toothbrushes and some cleaning solution. The next time it happens, the whole class will be staying in."

"Yes, sir," I shot back.

"That's not fair," Kevin shouted out in a nasally, whiny voice.

"Did someone tell you that life was fair, Mr. Boyez?" Mr. Manlin barked, cocking his head like he was extremely interested in the answer.

"No, sir," Kevin answered back. I almost fell off my chair.

Luckily, it was time to go to gym. But the walk over was not too cool. See, in our school, word travels faster than an airborne germ. Apparently, news of me dumping Julie's desk had already spread, because on my way to the playground some little second-grader passed me in the hallway, called me a boogie nose, and kicked me in the shins. "That was Julie's little sister," Matt informed me as I rubbed my shin.

All the girls were on my case at recess. They were saying that I was a male chauvinist because I expected a girl to clean better than a guy. I tried to convince them that Mr. Manlin was the male chauvinist, not me, but they didn't buy it. I decided I would never dump another girl's desk again.

Larry was not a happy camper. We were all gathered around the basketball court and he came barging into the middle of our game and said he had something really important to tell us.

"This ought to be good," Jax said to me. "Maybe he's going to do us all a favor and join the circus."

I wanted to get back on Jax's good side, so I shook my head like I was one of the good guys. We all stopped playing and gathered around to hear.

Larry forced his arm around my shoulder and Matt's neck, then pulled everyone into a circle. "Remember when I told you that my mom's brother, Uncle Butch, wasn't going to be too happy when he heard how the sergeant's been treating me?"

We all looked at each other.

"Well," he continued in a whisper, "Uncle Butch is going to pay Mr. Manlin a little visit today after school. He doesn't even know yet about what Mr. Manlin did to me this morning."

"Big deal," Jax said. "I think that's called a conference."

Larry shook his head defiantly. "You don't get it, Jax. Uncle Butch doesn't take anything from anyone. Even my bedroom's been clean since he showed up. He's not about to let that guy push around his favorite nephew. Just wait. You'll see him for yourself. He's coming today after school at three-fifteen."

None of us really believed it. I mean, what was the guy going to do, punch out his lights? Plus, I had no doubt that Mr. Manlin could take care of himself. He could just give someone a certain look and break them down.

So, after recess, the day went on pretty much as usual. At 3:10 the principal came on the intercom. "Well, hello out there in Wild Boar land. I hope everyone has had a good day. First I would like to announce that the winner of the ice cream party is Mrs. Tally's second-grade class. Congratulations for collecting the highest percentage of PTO membership dues in the school. And now, let's have the walkers to the gym."

Everyone ran to get their book bags. Then we heard more static come on the intercom, then, "Oh, Mr. Manlin, could you please tell Lauren she's taking the bus today, and there's a Mr. Butch Wood waiting in my office to see you. May I send him down now?"

"Absolutely," Mr. Manlin replied. He didn't look one bit scared or concerned.

On the way out the door, Mr. Manlin reminded everyone to bring in clay on Monday for our science experiment. "We are going to be making volcanoes."

Larry poked me in the back and whispered, "It's D day for the sergeant." I looked at Matt and Jax. Maybe Larry wasn't just a lot of talk after all.

When our bus was called, we all marched down the hall in single file until we were out of Mr. Manlin's sight. Then we ran so we'd get a seat at the back of the bus. While running, the three of us almost crashed into this huge creature that bore a striking resemblance to the Incredible Hulk. He slapped Larry a high five as we passed. "Uncle Butch, I presume," Jax stated matter-of-factly.

"Uncle Butch." Larry nodded, sneering.

Our mouths dropped opened. Larry wasn't exaggerating. The guy had a neck like a tree trunk and a gnarled, scarred face that could scare off a Doberman.

"What do you think?" Chris asked me, his eyes popping.

"I don't know," I replied. "The guy did look like he was in a bad mood." You know, for a minute there, I almost felt sorry for Mr. Manlin.

On the bus we all took bets on who would be the winner if they got into a fight. Everyone thought it would be Butch, but I had my money on Mr. Manlin.

4.
Mrs. Sweetwater

When Monday morning rolled around, for the first time this year I was looking forward to going to school. If I was right, Chris, Matt, and Jax owed me two dollars each. If I was wrong, I'd be out six bucks.

On the bus Matt said that he bet Mr. Manlin would at least have a black eye or something. Chris said he was a goner, and Jax said she didn't want to comment. We'd find out soon enough.

So we all hurried into the classroom, and guess what? No Mr. Manlin. Instead, there was a substitute sitting in his spot. She had already written her name on the blackboard: Mrs. Sweetwater. The woman looked to be about sixty-five — maybe even older — with short dyed red hair and small, wire-rimmed glasses that sat on the end of her nose. The funny part was that even Larry looked surprised.

The bell rang at 9:00 and everybody got really quiet. Mrs. Sweetwater stood up in front of the class and said, "Good morning. My name is Mrs. Sweetwater, and I'll be your substitute teacher for a while." She had this annoying voice that sounded like she was holding her nose when she spoke. "Now, Mr. Manlin had to leave suddenly, so he didn't get a chance to tell me much about anything. I'm going to have to rely on all of you to show me the ropes."

At first I thought maybe this was some kind of trick or test. Maybe Mr. Manlin had just planted her in our class for a day to see if we would follow all the rules and procedures he'd drilled into us for the last two weeks. I wasn't about to take any chances. Not at first, anyway.

Mrs. Sweetwater asked if someone would take roll call. Jax must have been thinking the same thing I was, because she raised her hand and said, "That's my job." Walking to the front of the class, she proceeded to call out everyone's name. There was only one person absent. "I'm going to deliver this to the office," Jax said. "I'll be right back."

Larry raised his hand next.

She pointed to him and asked, "And you are?"

"Lawrence Hensack, this week's class leader."

We all started laughing really hard, but Mrs. Sweetwater said she would not tolerate impoliteness and told us to be quiet while he spoke.

The class got quiet because everyone wanted to hear what he was going to come out with next.

Larry continued. "Mr. Manlin appointed me

class leader this week, so I just wanted you to know that if you need to ask how things are done you can count on me."

Mrs. Sweetwater looked pleased. "Why, thank you, Lawrence. That's nice to know."

Becca raised her hand. "Where is Mr. Manlin and when will he be back?"

"Oh, I don't really know," Mrs. Sweetwater said. "All I know is that I'm to come in here every day until they tell me not to. I believe your principal, Mr. Carson, will be in at the end of the week to talk to all of you."

"You mean he could be gone all week?" I asked, trying not to sound too thrilled.

"Yes. Maybe longer. But I'll let Mr. Carson explain it to you. Now, Lawrence, what do you usually start with in the morning?"

"A song," Larry said with a straight face. "Mr. Manlin says it gets the day off on a cheerful note."

We all kind of exchanged funny looks. Larry was grinning from ear to ear.

"Okay," Mrs. Sweetwater said, looking at Larry. "How about if you get us started. Then we'll all sing along."

Larry ran and grabbed a banana from Matt's lunch box, then started peeling it and dancing around like some Latin rumba man, belting out:

> "I'm a Chiquita Banana
> And I'm here to say

29

If you want to get your teacher
There's an easy way.
Just peel a banana and
Drop it on the floor
And watch your teacher go
We-e-e-e-e! Out the door."

Then Larry took a little bow. The whole class was laughing their heads off, but clearly Mrs. Sweetwater was not amused. "Please have a seat, Lawrence," she said in a very controlled, measured voice that sounded much meaner and definitely crankier than a few minutes ago.

Meanwhile, out of the corner of my eye I saw Kevin starting to open the window next to his desk. About thirty seconds later, I saw Kevin actually slip out of the window. Mrs. Sweetwater must not have noticed, because she told us all to open up our science books to the fourth chapter. We would postpone Mr. Manlin's volcano experiment for a while.

I could hardly wait until recess to discuss what had really happened to Mr. Manlin. Larry kept giving me this "I told you so" look, but I wasn't convinced until I heard the story.

We all gathered by the field and huddled around Larry. I could tell by the way he was acting that he thought he was really hot stuff now.

Larry said, "I know you guys didn't believe me

when I told you my uncle Butch would set the sergeant straight, but now you can see for yourselves."

"How do we know you're not just lying, Larry?" I asked. "Maybe it's just a coincidence that your uncle came in and then Mr. Manlin had to leave that night."

Larry got this smirk on his face, took out his comb, and slicked back his greasy hair. "Uncle Butch had a little talk with Mr. Manlin just like I told you he would. I don't think we'll have to worry about anything for a long, long time."

Jax shook her head. "I find it kind of hard to believe that Mr. Manlin would be afraid of your uncle Butch. Are you trying to say that he scared him out of town or —"

I broke in. "Now, Larry, what exactly did happen after school on Friday?"

Larry puffed up his chest like a peacock. "My uncle Butch didn't say much. Actually, he was out of town this weekend, so I didn't exactly get to talk to him. But you can only imagine what must have happened."

"Maybe he got sick or something," I said.

"Think what you want," Larry sneered. "But just remember that nobody messes with Larry Hensack and gets away with it." He held up both arms and made a muscle like only a jerk would do. Larry then strutted over to the basketball hoop and took a shot but missed.

"Poor Mr. Manlin," Jax said to the rest of us, still stunned.

"For all we know," Matt said, "maybe he got knocked in the head and he's wandering around the streets with amnesia."

I felt bad. But I couldn't say I was sorry he was gone.

Before we knew it, the bell rang and it was time for Mrs. Sweetwater again. We were taking full advantage of the poor substitute. By the end of the week, Mrs. Sweetwater was beginning to look like Wile E. Coyote after a few failed attempts to outsmart the Road Runner. Her short red hair was frizzed out and sticking up on the top of her head. Plus, I noticed that every once in a while she would bang her fists on the blackboard and mumble something indiscernible. Every day she'd start by saying, "Class, today is a new day, and a chance to start over on the right foot. I'm expecting all of you to give me your full attention."

Well, on about the fourth day, Jax stood up and took roll call as usual. When Jax returned from the office Mrs. Sweetwater said she'd decided to do things a little differently today and begin with a reading.

She stood in front of the class, leaned on her desk, and asked us all to open our books to chapter one of *Matilda*.

For the first few minutes, it seemed like everyone was cooperating. When it was my turn, I stood up, cleared my throat, and began reading — when all of a sudden I felt this big, wet *splat* hit me in the back. I jumped about a mile high, threw my book down on the desk, and screamed. Kevin was laughing so hard I thought he was going to fall off his chair.

Mrs. Sweetwater only took a few seconds to figure out that Kevin had blasted me with a water balloon from across the room. Water was everywhere.

"You jerk!" I screamed at Kevin.

Mrs. Sweetwater whizzed over to Kevin's desk, pulled him up by the arms, and said, "I demand an explanation."

The whole class got real quiet waiting to hear what Kevin had to say. He was just standing there, staring down at his feet, and mumbled, "Eric dared me to do it."

Mrs. Sweetwater's face and neck had broken out in these red splotches. In a very slow, controlled voice she said, "Kevin, if your brother dared you to jump off a bridge or out of a window, would you do it?"

Kevin was still looking down at his shoes, so Mrs. Sweetwater put her hand under his chin and raised his face so she could look him right in the eyes. "I demand an answer."

Kevin just shrugged. Then we all heard Larry yell, "Hey, Kevin, I dare you to jump out a window." Kevin looked over at him, then at Eric, then walked over to one of the classroom windows, opened it, and jumped out! He made this screaming sound like he'd fallen fifteen stories and made the scream sound real low at the end. Well, everyone in the class knew that it was only about twelve inches from the window to the ground. Our substitute obviously didn't.

"Oh my gosh!" Mrs. Sweetwater screamed, running to the window. The whole class leaned out the window and looked down to see Kevin crouched in the mud with this stupid smirk on his face. Before Mrs. Sweetwater got a chance to let him have it, we heard the classroom door open and then the booming voice of our principal, Mr. Carson.

Everyone ran back to their seats and Mrs. Sweetwater shut the window, leaving Kevin outside in the dirt. I think she didn't want to look like she couldn't handle us in front of the principal.

Mr. Carson gave us a questioning look, but Mrs. Sweetwater just smoothed down her hair and said, "Good morning, Mr. Carson."

"Good morning. If you don't mind, Mrs. Sweetwater, I'd like to have a few words with your class."

"Be my guest," she said, giving the rest of us a dirty look.

Mr. Carson leaned against the front of Mrs. Sweetwater's desk and gave us all the once-over.

"As you all know, Mr. Manlin has been absent for the past week and you have all had the privilege of working with Mrs. Sweetwater, who was kind enough to be coaxed out of retirement and fill in for us while Mr. Manlin is gone. I've chosen Mrs. Sweetwater because she is one of the finest teachers I know, and in fact, she taught my children when they attended this school many years ago. This woman could teach a rock to read. I expect everyone to give her your full cooperation."

He turned around and smiled at Mrs. Sweetwater, then continued. "Now, I'm sure you are all wondering what happened to Mr. Manlin, when he'll be returning, and all kinds of questions like that, right?"

"Right," we all answered.

"Well, Mr. Manlin was called off on a special assignment, which I am not at liberty to talk about, but I don't want any of you to be concerned. I assure you he is in perfect health and will be returning to this class shortly. I'm not sure exactly when, I can only say shortly. In the meantime, I'm sending a memo home to your parents explaining the temporary change. I'm confident each of you will carry on as Mr. Manlin would expect."

His eyes scanned over the room as he attempted to make eye contact with as many people as possible. Then he asked, "Can I count on that?"

"Yes, sir, Mr. Carson," most of us answered in a singsong tone.

"Good." He turned to Mrs. Sweetwater. "Let me know if there's any trouble."

He wasn't out of the room two minutes when there was a tapping on the window. I looked over and Kevin had his muddy hands and nose pressed against the glass like he was some kind of maniac. Everybody was laughing except Mrs. Sweetwater. Mrs. Sweetwater just looked at him, then calmly walked over, opened the window, and said, "Get back in here and stay in. And that includes recess. All next week."

By the time recess rolled around, we could hardly contain our joy at the prospect of Mr. Manlin's sudden departure and at our good luck to have gotten the retired Mrs. Sweetwater as his replacement.

As for me, I no longer had to worry about anyone wanting to keep a desk messy. I decided right there, from now on, everyone would pass my inspection.

School was starting to feel like one big party, with Larry handing out goodie bags in the form of jokes and pranks every day. Mrs. Sweetwater was starting to catch on a little since Kevin jumped out the window, but basically it was a free-for-all.

Desk inspection was a piece of cake. I let everyone pass, even some that would be considered only marginally neat. We started to have a little bug problem by the end of Mrs. Sweetwater's second week from all the candy and leftovers we stored in our desks, but mostly we just stepped on the bugs and kept on snacking!

The biggest difference I saw in Mrs. Sweetwater was that she wasn't as sweet as she first appeared to be. In fact, she was really cranky and in a bad mood. One morning, I thought she was winking at me. Then Jax and Matt thought the same thing. We realized she had developed a nervous tic in her right eye. It was a little scary, but then I got used to the tic and it didn't bother me anymore.

That Friday in science class, Mrs. Sweetwater asked us to pick a lab partner for our experiment. I picked Jax before Becca could get her.

"Okay," Mrs. Sweetwater said, holding up a test tube half filled with vinegar in one hand and a vial of baking soda in the other. "What we're going to do today is study chemical reactions that take place in nature. It is *very* important that you do not hold down the test tube cap with your finger. And once it's mixed, do not, I repeat, *do not* put the cap on and hold it down with your finger or we could have a serious explosion."

I saw the gleam in Kevin's eye the minute she said the word *explosion.*

"Now we'll add a touch of red dye to everyone's mixture to make it look like a real volcano," she continued. "I need two volunteers to walk around the room to make sure that each group understands what to do." Matt and I volunteered.

The two of us hadn't even made it to the first group when we saw Kevin and Eric wildly shaking the test tube and Kevin pressing down the cap with his finger. The word "Begin" had hardly left Mrs. Sweetwater's lips before red stuff was flying everywhere. Then Larry and his partner did the same and the cap exploded off and hit Mrs. Sweetwater in the eyebrow. She let out a horrible scream and things just went downhill from there.

Luckily, no one was seriously hurt, but half the class was covered in red dye and our substitute looked like she had stuck her finger in an electrical socket.

Mrs. Sweetwater was speechless. She left the room and returned shortly with a small Band-Aid on her eyebrow. She was probably too tired to think about too much more than just surviving another day with us. Clearly, we had worn her down. She looked like she had aged ten years in the two short weeks she had been with us.

That was the last time we ever saw Mrs. Sweetwater. In some ways, I was really sorry to see her go. I didn't think that school could be any better — even if I had gotten Mrs. Smith for a fifth-grade teacher. I was only hoping the next substitute would be as nice.

5.
Sheriff Hester

After the way I had been dreading the fifth grade, it was turning out to be my most fun year ever. School was becoming almost more exciting than my weekends — just thinking about who the next substitute would be and what we'd get away with. I never knew what was going to happen next.

The Monday after the volcano incident, I didn't take the bus to school. My mom had a day off and she wanted to drive me so we could have a chance to talk. Mostly she wanted to know how everything was going, and if I minded having a substitute and stuff like that. I told her I actually liked it and I was having my best year ever. I even gave her a kiss before I got out of the car, which I think really shocked her.

I walked into the classroom and looked over at the teacher's desk. The chair was empty. That was our cue to just relax and be ourselves.

Everybody was talking and being really rambunctious. A couple of kids were wrestling on the floor and throwing lunch bags when all of a sudden, the classroom door flew open. In burst this guy who looked mean and angry before we even did anything to make him that way. He was about six feet two with a handlebar mustache and squinty brown eyes that zipped everywhere. He was wearing a cowboy hat and giant cowboy boots that were so pointed a bug in the corner couldn't escape him. I knew that shoe feature would really come in handy in our class. And his legs were a little bowed, like someone who's been riding a horse too long.

The man grabbed a chair, whirled it around, and straddled it so he could sit facing us. He put his elbows on the back while he rolled his hat brim in his hands. Then he gave us a long laser-like stare and shouted, "There's a new sheriff in town and we're not doing business the old way!" He had the thickest Southern accent I had ever heard. He drew all his words out like he was pulling taffy.

The class got so quiet you could only hear the sounds of rhythmic breathing. No one moved. I glanced over at Larry, and even he looked scared. I was sure the guy was crazy.

Next thing, the new sheriff stomped over to the blackboard and wrote *Mr. Hester* in giant letters so hard the chalk broke in two. When he was finished, he gave us that stare again and said, "Mrs. Sweetwater won't be returning. The party is over. We're doing things my way now, and if anyone has a problem with that I'd like to know about it."

Silence.

"Okay, then, just to be sure we're all speaking the same language here, I'll start by telling you the rules. Number one: I'm in charge, and you're not. Anyone gives me trouble and they can expect double trouble in return. You misbehave, you pay. You try to pull a fast one, I'll be faster. You try the old slip out the window routine, I'll form a posse to find you. And I *will* find you."

"What happens when you find someone?" I asked curiously.

He glared at me. "What do you think? Jail, of course." As if on cue, the classroom door flew open and in walked these two guys carrying what looked like a giant cardboard box, like the ones refrigerators come in. "Put it in the corner, boys."

I turned around to look at the massive carton. The box had "County Jail" written in Magic Marker across the top and a window cut out in the front with bars made out of giant rubber bands.

The sheriff patted his vest and continued, "I was born and bred on the mean Texas plains, and I can break in a wild pony faster than you can say rattlesnake. You young cowpokes think I'm not on to you? Think again. Ever hear of the S.O.S. club?"

We shook our heads and looked at each other. "What's S.O.S. stand for?" Larry shouted out.

Sheriff Hester smirked. "S.O.S. stands for the Society of Substitutes. We stick together and watch out for one another. See, I had the lowdown on y'all from Mrs. Sweetwater. She's resting comfortably now. She told me about all your antics, and I'm ready to play hardball." He twirled the ends of his mustache. "In other words, I've got your number, and your number's up."

With that, Class 512 began another exciting adventure. I think everyone got used to Mr. Hester's rodeo-style classroom. He referred to the girls as "ma'am" and the boys as "pardner" and appointed someone his assistant deputy every day. Actually, he even made English class fun. We'd make a pretend campfire and eat marshmallows off sticks while we discussed the theme and characters in a book we were reading, *Red River Valley*.

Once Larry got put in the slammer for putting a few marshmallows on the sheriff's chair, but Larry said sitting in that box was like having his own apartment. Mr. Hester had trouble getting him to come out when the buses were called.

You know, Mr. Hester wasn't really a bad guy. Once he felt he'd let us know who was in charge, he began to relax a little. In the few short days he was with us, he started to be a fun guy.

One day, when we were all getting a little rowdy, he decided to take us outside for a game of baseball. He let us pick teams, the Rustlers against the Outlaws. There was one big blonde girl in our class. Mr. Hester made her the pitcher. She was the tallest girl in the fifth grade and was built like an American Gladiator.

Mr. Hester didn't know it, but this girl could pitch one powerful ball. Well, Mr. Hester was first to go up to bat. The first ball went over his head, but the next ball plowed him right between the eyes. We all watched his eyes cross, then they glazed over and he passed out cold.

One of the teachers must have seen it from a window, because before we knew it, the ambulance was there, and they were carrying away poor Mr. Hester.

The last thing I remember was the sight of Sheriff Hester being lifted onto the stretcher and the sound of the ambulance siren as it drove off and slowly faded into the distance.

Our principal came in the following morning with Mr. Thompson, the art teacher, and we all made this giant get well card to send to Mr. Hester. Everyone signed it and wrote their own special get well message. Strangely enough, the card came back two days later marked *Return to sender, address unknown*.

You could say the year was turning out to be like one big, exciting baseball game, and the score was a real washout: Class 512–3, Substitutes–0. We just couldn't wait to see who would be the next poor, unsuspecting batter.

6.
The Milder Ms. Wilder

She was almost too good to be true. I think even Larry Hensack felt a tinge of guilt when our next substitute, Ms. Wilder, stepped unsuspectingly into our classroom.

As she stood in front of the class, wearing a little red checkered blouse and pleated skirt, we knew we were in complete control. I overheard Kevin whisper to his brother, "This one's gonna be too easy — not even a challenge." Then they both snickered with delight.

The class was being pretty noisy. Ms. Wilder cleared her throat twice, trying to get our attention. That didn't work. "Class, please, class, please!" she said in this soft little voice that didn't stand a chance.

Finally, Jax stood up and yelled at the top of her lungs, "SHUT UP!" Now *that* got everyone's attention, because Jax was usually pretty quiet.

Ms. Wilder's eyes grew really wide as they looked over the class, then zeroed in on Jax.

"Thank you. My name is Ms. Mildred Wilder. As you've probably figured out by now, I'm your new substitute teacher. Now, I'd like to start out by telling you something about myself. Then I'd like to know something about each one of you."

She continued in her sugary little voice, "So, first, I'll start with me. I graduated from the University of Delaware with a degree in social studies. I did my student teaching here in Mrs. Smith's class. Most importantly, I'm very, very excited to be here," she gushed. She took a sip of tea from the mug on her desk. "Basically, I feel my goal here is for you to learn something. Most of all, we're going to have fun doing it." She clapped her hands together in enthusiasm.

Matt's hand shot up like a rocket.

"Please stand and tell me your name, sir," Ms. Wilder said.

"Matt Kalil," he stated. "I just want to know how you feel about homework?"

"It's optional." She shrugged as if homework was no big deal.

Next, Chris raised his hand. "You mean we don't have to do it if we don't want to?"

"Exactly."

"Wouldn't we all fail if we didn't study?" Chris asked.

"Most likely," Ms. Wilder agreed. "But don't you think you should have a choice?"

I looked around the room. Everyone had this gleeful but dumbfounded expression on their faces.

"Let's put it this way, class," she said. "I'm not here to baby-sit. I'm here to teach those of you who would like to learn. I know that's the reason we're all here. Right? By the time one reaches the fifth grade, I think you should be responsible enough to make your own decisions. Entertain your brain and your brain will be pleased, I always say."

She put her hands above her head and did a ballerina spin. "One thing I will tell you is that I am very big on real-life educational experiences. Getting out there and really doing it is one of the most educational tools for young people. So as long as I'm here, I'm going to try and give you as many experiences as possible. Picnics, trips, outdoor educational games. We're not going to watch life from the sidelines. We're going to be doers!"

"This must be Christmas," Larry whispered under his breath, then shouted out, "Welcome, Mrs. Wilder!" Bad move.

Without warning, some alien creature seemed to enter her body and Ms. Wilder's face transformed before our eyes. Her face turned a dark shade of purple, and the veins in her neck popped up like toast. Her eyes rolled around eerily in their sockets. Through clenched teeth she

47

sneered, "My name is Ms. Mildred Wilder. *Not* Mrs. Wilder. *Not* Mrs. Millie Wilder. *Not* Millie Wilder. *Not* Ms. Millie. It's Ms. Mildred Wilder!" She eyeballed each and every one of us, then continued in an even deeper, shakier voice.

"You respect my name, I'll respect yours. And we'll all get along just fine. Just peachy." Then, just like that, her voice got sweet and she was smiling again. "Now, did you have a question, Larry?"

Bizarre wasn't the word for what had happened. Maybe we had gone too far. Maybe we had actually pushed her over that edge. But really, what was the big deal? All Larry did was shout and slightly mess up her name. Then it hit me. Maybe she belonged to that S.O.S. substitute teacher's club Mr. Hester had told us about. She probably had heard about our reputation ahead of time.

"Any further questions?" she asked.

We all shook our heads.

"Well, then, there are just two more things I would like you to know about me," she added, holding up two fingers. "One, I'm very much into health. I believe the body must be nourished continually in order to feed the mind. Therefore, I am a proponent of healthy eating in my classroom anytime you feel your body needs nourishment. I myself will eat when my body tells me it's time.

I only ask that when you do, it's something healthy."

She proceeded to bring out this see-through container filled with what looked like mud. "Smashed figs and whole grains," she announced, dipping in a spoon and stuffing her mouth, rolling her eyes up in pleasure, smacking her lips.

"The second thing is, I strongly believe in the power of song." She put her hands up like a ballerina and twirled around again, singing, "La, la, la, la. Nothing lifts the spirits and feeds the heart like singing. There will be many opportunities when I will ask you to sing something instead of say it."

Kevin raised his hand and sang to the tune of "Yankee Doodle Dandy," "I have to go-o to the bath . . . room! I . . . really . . . really have to go-o!" A few people snickered.

But Ms. Wilder looked pleased and sang back, "Do-oo what you got to do-oo." The tune was unidentifiable, but the voice was this horrible, screechy, high-pitched shriek, worse than listening to nails scraping against the blackboard.

I think on that first day we just chalked it up to her being a little odd. I mean, how could we have known how disturbed she really was? Because that day was to be the first small clue that she might be more than slightly cracked. The Milder

Mrs. Wilder — I mean Ms. Wilder — was anything but mild.

In fact, she had begun to stroll down that loony yellow brick road long before she came into Class 512. We were just the final pit stop on her way to see the wizard. No doubt she planned to ask him for a normal brain.

7.
A Class Act

After that first day, Ms. Wilder seemed to calm down a bit. The following week was the most fun I'd had in school since kindergarten. Basically, we were running the show, and the funny part was, Ms. Wilder didn't even seem to notice.

At recess that week, we took a vote and re-elected our class officials, just like with Mr. Manlin. Only the titles were slightly different.

The kids voted Matt Class Leader. Matt took it upon himself to hand out homework assignments that day at lunch. That's when we really started to discover how much talent we had in our classroom.

The first assignment he gave was that every kid was to make a "KICK ME" sign that night for Ms. Wilder to wear. While most of the kids did just simple "KICK ME" ones with a little smiley face, Kevin's were much wittier and creative. So the class voted him Official Sign Maker. The kid had a real artistic streak that no one had ever known about.

We sort of fell into a routine. Each morning Kevin would come in with a new creative slogan to stick on Ms. Wilder. His range of names was really quite impressive, everything from Ms. Millie the Hillbilly from Chile to Silly Mrs. Millie to Millie Vanilli. Plus, they were all accompanied by these funny little cartoon drawings.

In addition, Larry was voted Official Sticker Man. His job was to sneak up and stick the sign on her each morning. He would remove it before she had lunch with the faculty. Sometimes he'd stick the morning sign back on after lunch. Or, if Kevin was in a real creative mood that day, she'd get an entirely new one. He kept all of the signs in a secret hiding place in the classroom.

As for me, I continued on in my role as Chief Inspector. Only my requirements for a desk being "up to standard," as Mr. Manlin would say, took on a whole new meaning.

In order to pass desk inspection, each student had to have an interesting variety of snacks, insects, games, or live animals on hand. In fact, within a week we pretty much had our own wildlife zoo living inside our desks.

Chris' was the best. He had a baby iguana living in his, which we made our class mascot. We named him Willy. The following day, we decided that Willy was lonely living in there all by himself, and Eric brought him a wife. We, of course, named her Milly.

The one thing none of us counted on was just how fast iguanas grew. Not to mention how much they ate! When Willy and Milly were first brought in, they were both only about six inches long.

They seemed to be growing an inch a day, and we didn't know how much longer we could keep them in their cage inside Chris's desk. It was getting tough to keep them supplied with lettuce and vegetables.

Jax brought in a gecko, this creature her cousin gave her that her mother didn't want in the house. We named it Egor. Mostly we fed it flies, since there were so many around with all the food and stuff. The crickets had to be imported from someone's backyard. Between the gecko and the iguanas, our food supplies were dwindling. But by the end of the week, we had all gotten pretty attached to old Willy and Milly and Egor.

The most unbelievable part was that on Friday morning, Ms. Wilder announced that she had a little surprise for us. We thought it would be an ice cream treat or maybe a movie. Nobody could wait to hear. We were sitting on the edge of our seats when she finally told us.

"Next Tuesday," Ms. Wilder announced, "I will be taking all of you on a little picnic."

We all got so excited and noisy, she blinked the

53

lights on and off until we quieted down. "Now, if you'll let me continue, thank you. You don't have to worry about lunch, I'm taking care of everything. The only thing I want you to do is have a good time." She clapped her hands together and jumped up and down.

"Okay, I've got permission slips that must be signed over the weekend and returned to me on Monday."

I raised my hand. "Where is this picnic going to be?"

She smiled sweetly. "Well, it is a surprise, but I will tell you we're going to Hershey, Pennsylvania. I'd like you all to dress in casual clothes that you wouldn't mind getting dirty or torn."

Matt raised his hand and asked what everybody was thinking. "It's Hershey Park, right?"

Ms. Wilder just pretended to pull a zipper across her lips. "No more hints. It's a surprise."

I couldn't believe my luck. Hershey Park was one of my most favorite places on earth! I still have dreams about riding the Sidewinder, the most thrilling roller coaster known to man. Not to mention stuffing my mouth with all those delicious Hershey chocolate bars and Twizzlers!

Later that afternoon, Ms. Wilder had to go into a meeting, so she gave us a forty-five-minute study period. Right before she left the room, she said she hoped she could trust us to use our time wisely. She'd be back before the principal's end-of-day announcements. We all assured her we could be trusted.

After she left, we waited a good five minutes. Kevin had lookout duty that day. He checked out the hallway to make sure the coast was clear, then gave the thumbs-up sign. It was time for the Reptile Olympics!

Larry and Eric took Willy and Milly and Egor out of the desks and let them get a good stretch before the run. The whole thing was so cool. We drew a starting line and finishing line on the floor, taping down racing lanes between the desks. We put all the reptiles at the starting mark. Then we put several flies, crickets, and vegetable sticks at the finish line.

I was the announcer, so I made a little megaphone out of a piece of paper. Jax and Becca gave the starting signal and Milly and Willy took off like race cars. Egor went the wrong way. We were all screaming and yelling when Kevin signaled that Ms. Wilder was on her way back. We quickly stuck Willy, Milly, and Egor back in the desks and everyone pretended to be studying when she walked into the room twenty minutes early. It was a close call!

She took a seat at her desk and announced a pop quiz.

I raised my hand. "You're just kidding, right?"

Need I say, not one person passed.

8.
The Quiz

When I walked into the classroom on Monday morning, Ms. Wilder was humming and writing at her desk. She seemed to be in a particularly good mood. Everyone was so excited about going to Hershey Park the following day, we could hardly stay in our seats. As soon as roll call was over, she told the class that she had another little surprise for us. That woman was full of surprises.

"Now, close your eyes," she sang. I could hear her scurrying around the room doing something.

"Okay, you can open them now," she said a few minutes later. I looked up and put my hand to my mouth in horror. Right there in front of our very eyes was a collection of all the signs Ms. Wilder had worn over the past two weeks. They were neatly mounted on a piece of neon orange poster board.

"Would anyone like to claim credit for these lovely pieces of art?" she asked. Her face turned red, and her eyes were wild and bulging. She was holding the poster board so tight, her knuckles were as white as snowballs.

Silence.

"C'mon. Don't be shy. I never knew how much talent and energy you kids could put into a project when you really set your minds to it."

Nobody said a word.

"Well, that's too bad," she said calmly. "Now the whole class must suffer. But I want you to know that I, too, have a wonderful sense of humor." She laughed wickedly, but continued to laugh way too hard for way too long. When she finally stopped, her eyes narrowed into beady little slits and her tongue was darting in and out of her mouth like a snake. I got a shiver down my spine.

Pacing up and down the aisle like a wild animal, she hissed, "I want each of you to write each sign one hundred times for homework tonight. Have it on my desk first thing in the morning. Oh, and don't forget to accompany each sign with the beautifully detailed artwork. If anyone has a problem with completing this assignment, I would like a note from your parents explaining why."

Right before recess, she had Jax pass out a tray of health food she had whipped up the night before. Smashed figs rolled in bits of nuts and cheese. They smelled like stinky sneaker feet. Nobody dared to refuse. Everyone took one and popped it in their mouths, trying to swallow without tasting.

We had to stay in from recess, writing down the signs and drawing the pictures we would have to duplicate. If I was lucky I'd get an hour's sleep that night. I figured I would have to spend every waking moment writing Ms. Wilder's nicknames and duplicating Kevin's stupid drawings.

The torture continued. That afternoon, Ms. Wilder pulled a surprise social studies quiz. This was getting to be a bad habit of hers. She graded them on the spot, then had Matt pass them back to everyone. I could hear moaning all around the room. After all the papers were passed out, Ms. Wilder said that there was only one A in the entire class.

I felt like reporting her because, number one, Mr. Manlin never did that, and two, I got a D. This was on top of the quiz I had failed last Friday. I knew my dad would freak. Worse, I could see my dirt bike disintegrating into a pile of dust before my very eyes.

I raised my hand. "There must be some mistake, Ms. Wilder," I said. "See, I'm pretty much a straight-A kind of guy, so if I got a D no one else even had a chance. Could we please take the test over so I won't have to bring this home and upset my parents?"

She smiled. "The mistake is that you didn't study when I gave you the opportunity. Please be quiet, Mr. Malloy. I have an announcement to make. I want all of your social studies tests signed by your parents tonight and on my desk in the morning before we leave on our picnic. No signatures, no picky-nicky."

The principal came on the intercom and called out the buses. We ran out and I caught up with Matt and Chris. "What did you guys get on your test?" I asked.

"I got a D," Matt said.

"F," Chris groaned.

"What are your parents going to say?"

Matt shook his head. "They won't be too happy."

"My parents will ground me," Chris said.

"My dad's going to flip. I can't have him sign this," I said.

We all got off the bus at my house. My mom had just gotten home from work. She gave us some snacks and we took them up in the tree house with us along with our book bags.

"Hey, dweebs," I heard from down below.

"That's got to be Dillon and Weasel."

"Hey," we shouted back.

We heard one of them start up the ladder. Weasel. "So, I hear you guys lucked out and got another substitute."

"Yeah," Chris said, "but we've also got big problems. She pulled another surprise test on us today and none of us did very well."

"So?"

"So," I said, "this time the tests have to be signed by our parents and returned in the morning."

"What did you get, Jeff?" my brother asked. "Don't tell me it wasn't your standard A plus?"

"No, it was your basic D. Dad's going to kill me."

"You're right. I wouldn't want to be you tonight," Dillon agreed. "And there goes your dirt bike."

"Not necessarily," Weasel said, wiggling his eyebrows up and down.

"What do you mean?" I asked.

"Haven't you ever heard of 'artistic license'?" Weasel asked me.

"What's that?" Matt crinkled up his face.

"Trouble, I'm sure," I said to Matt. But we were all so desperate we were even willing to listen to a guy like Weasel.

"See, you just take the D and with a little curl of the pen, you turn it into a B. Magic brains."

"Yeah, well, what happens when you turn it back in to your teacher and she sees you've changed the grade?"

"That's easy. You just use erasable ink. Voilà. In the morning it's a D again."

"And just where are we going to get erasable ink?" Matt asked.

"From your good friend and buddy, The Weez.

I happen to keep it in my book bag, which is sitting in your den as we speak. Where have you guys been? Erasable ink is almost as vital to your learning years as oxygen."

Weasel ran inside my house and came back a minute later with a pen.

"You first," I said to Matt.

Matt took the pen and began his work. When he finished, we all looked at his new B like he had performed some miracle surgery or something.

"Not bad," Weasel admired. "Hardly detectable even to the trained eye." Dillon was pretty quiet the whole time. I think he didn't really want to be a part of it in case we got caught.

So, one by one, we all went from dumbbell to scholar with the mere flick of a pen.

I'd like to say that I gave the matter a lot of thought, but I did say to myself I would do it just this once. I figured if I pulled A's on the rest of the tests it would all average out and nobody would ever know. All I could think about at the time was losing my dirt bike and getting grounded. I hoped this wasn't how criminals started out. I got my dad to sign it as soon as he came home from work. I couldn't look him in the eye when he said, "Pretty good job."

Well, that night I think I was somewhere around writing the eightieth Ms. Millie Vanilli when it finally hit me. Wasn't Ms. Wilder the substitute Weasel and Dillon had mentioned at the beginning of the school year?

I went running out of my room and banged on Dillon's bedroom door.

"What do you want?" he screamed. "I'm on the phone."

"It's urgent. Can I come in?" I figured he was probably talking to his girlfriend, but I went in anyway without waiting for an answer.

He put his hand over the mouthpiece. "What?"

"Remember that substitute you and Weasel mentioned one time, Ms. Wilder?"

"Yeah. What about her?"

"She's the one I've got for a substitute until Mr. Manlin returns. Do you think she's the type that would notice if a grade had been tampered with? You know, check for eraser marks or something?"

Dillon just looked at me. Then he started laughing so hard I thought he was going to fall off his bed.

"What's so funny?" I asked, hoping to get a clue.

When he finally stopped laughing, all he said was, "Nothing." Then he told me to get out and close his door. I know I heard him whisper something about Frankenstein into the phone to his girlfriend.

"C'mon, Dillon, just answer me this. Do you think that there might be something wrong with

that woman? You know, like she's got two per-
sonalities or something, like a Dr. Jekyll and Mr.
Hyde?"

"Two?" Dillon said in between choking laughs.
"Close my door, punk!"

I closed the door. Actually, I slammed it. I got a
sinking feeling in my stomach that kept me
awake until way after midnight. I was sorry I had
changed my grade. And not just because I could
get caught. I had always tried to be an honest
person. Plus, I was thinking about getting into
politics someday. I wouldn't want that on my
record. I could just hear my dad if he found out:
"Tell that to the judge."

The next morning on the bus, Matt, Chris, and
I sat together in the back. I had Weasel's erasable
ink pen, so I took out my signed test and went to
work immediately to change my B back to the
original D. Very carefully, I tried to erase the little curved line I had put in the middle of the D. To
my horror, the mark wasn't budging.

"You got it?" Matt asked, looking anxiously
over my shoulder.

"No," I snapped. "The mark isn't erasing."

"You're kidding us, right?" Chris said.

I tried even harder to erase it, but it was no
use. If I erased any harder, it was going to start
taking off the paper. "Guess what, guys, The
Weez has played a little joke. He must have

switched the erasable pen with a real one when we weren't paying attention." I felt sick to my stomach.

At that point we were all just hoping that Ms. Wilder didn't look at the test grades again before she slipped them back into our folders. I thought we had lucked out because nothing was ever mentioned.

9.
Sweet Revenge

That day everyone showed up exhausted with their signed permission slips, their one hundred signs, and about three blisters on each hand from duplicating the stupid signs. But we were all so excited about going to Hershey Park, everyone got recharged.

We began our morning as usual. Jax took roll call. But Kevin decided to skip the daily sign. No one wanted to jeopardize our day at Hershey Park.

The bus was already waiting when we lined up in the lobby. If you wanted to call it a bus. The clunker looked like some rickety old wreck that had been resurrected from the bus graveyard. The whole thing was painted a rusted mustard color, with "Wash Me" written in the dirt on the back window. Most of the seats were hacked and the stuffing was coming out of the cushions. I only hoped it would make the two-hour trip. I felt uneasy, but I soon forgot about it.

I checked my pockets getting on. I had eight dollars with me so I could bring home some chocolate and souvenirs. Matt and Chris each took five. Larry didn't bring any money, but he said that we each had to give him two dollars or he'd punch our lights out. I was so excited about everything, I didn't even mind handing over a few bucks.

The ride was so bumpy and the engine so loud, the trip seemed to take forever. Not to mention, none of the rusted windows would open and it was steaming hot inside the bus. "The first thing I'm heading for is the Sidewinder roller coaster," I yelled to Matt across the row.

"Oh, yeah," Matt said. "My brother said we can't miss the Dare Rider. He said it's awesome."

"We should try and convince Ms. Wilder to go on it with us," Larry snickered. "She'll be scared out of her wits. She probably won't be able to even talk for a few days."

"Maybe we shouldn't chance it," I said. "What if she had a heart attack and then we got a really mean substitute? Or worse, Mr. Manlin could come back sooner than he had planned."

"Yeah, you're right," Matt nodded. "We'll take it easy on the old girl."

"Well, I'm going to buy one of those twelve-pound candy bars. I could keep it in my desk and eat a little each day," I said, licking my lips.

After riding for about two hours, we felt like

we were suffocating. Larry finally managed to pry a window open with an old crowbar someone left under a seat. In floated the aroma of delicious sweet chocolate. Everyone's nostrils were flaring, sniffing the air like a pack of dogs.

"There it is!" Larry shouted. "Hershey Park. I'm ready for a ride on the wild side!"

Everyone was screaming and shouting and jumping up and down in their seats. "We're here! We're here!" The sweet aroma of chocolate was unbelievable.

"Hey," I shouted. "The bus driver is going too fast. He's going to have to slam on the brakes in order to make the turn into Hershey Park! Everybody hold on!" But he never turned. Moments later we realized we had driven past the entrance to Hershey Park and were still going at full speed down the highway.

"What gives?" Larry yelled to the bus driver, but he didn't answer. Instead, the bus driver just turned his head and glared at us with this mean, sinister grin. That was the first time we got a look at his face. He looked like he hadn't shaved in a week. He was missing his front teeth, and his eyes looked wild and crazed. I was sure he and Ms. Wilder winked at each other just then. My heart sank.

"Oh, no," I said to Matt and Kevin. "Maybe the two of them are in this together."

Suddenly the bus slowed, then came to a

screeching halt. We pulled into an overgrown, marshy-looking field. I looked out my window and saw a small wooden sign that read: HERSHEY PARKLANDS. My heart fell three stories.

Ms. Wilder stood up in the aisle and blew a whistle she had hanging from her neck. "We're here!" she announced with this wicked, sly smile. "Now, I would like everyone to follow me single file and form a circle when we get to our destination. I have a wonderful surprise for all of you."

I wondered why we were going to have to walk to Hershey Park when the bus driver could have just pulled up to the entrance and let us out.

We figured out very quickly that we weren't going to Hershey Park at all. Instead, Ms. Wilder led us through about a hundred feet of itchy high grass and muddy terrain swarming with gnats and insects. When she reached this scummy-looking pond, she spun around and made a stop gesture with her hands.

Next, Ms. Wilder did some kind of high shrill birdcall, and out of the high grasses emerged this nerdy, geeky-looking guy, skinny as a stick insect. In fact, he reminded me a little of a grasshopper. He had bulging eyes and thick glasses. He was wearing a goofy safari outfit and a straw hat and had binoculars hanging around his neck. He gave us a little salute and shouted, "Greetings, young nature enthusiasts."

Everyone moaned. Ms. Wilder blew the whistle so loud and long I worried I might go deaf. "Class," Ms. Wilder said, looking at the geek with admiration like he was some big Hollywood movie star, "I would like you all to have the privilege of meeting the brilliant and highly revered Professor Greenfeld." She applauded loudly. The class was silent. "Not only is he one of the world's experts on marshland grasses, but he's in charge of the very lands that we're standing on. As a personal favor to me, Professor Greenfeld has agreed to spend the day with us, explaining in detail each variety of grass that can be found here, their origins, and their role in America's future."

Everybody gave a disappointed moan. Kevin shouted out, "You've got to be kidding."

Ms. Wilder blew the whistle so hard my ears hurt. "What could be more exciting than your own private tour guide through some of the most unusual and exciting grasses in all of America?"

"Spending the day sticking bamboo shoots up my fingernails," Larry muttered under his breath. Ms. Wilder shot him a dirty look.

The next few hours were sheer agony, to say the least. Mr. Greenfeld introduced himself and told us in nauseating detail about each and every grass species we would encounter in our big adventure.

We found it hard to pay attention, as the horseflies and mosquitoes were diving at us left and right. Giant red welts began to appear on our arms and necks from the bites. When we finally did get a breeze, it carried the torturous aroma of chocolate. Some of us even started to drool.

Just when I thought there was nothing else that anyone could say about grass, the professor would ramble on for another twenty minutes. After an eternity, he said our adventure would begin. He wrapped it up with one final warning: *"Steer clear of the swamp. Fall in and you're history."*

Ms. Wilder stood up again and said, "Now, I know you are all wishing that we could spend a little time at Hershey Park. The professor and I have made up a little contest. If anyone here, on our adventure through the grasslands, can spot a yellow-bellied marsh-dweller, you will win an hour at Hershey Park for the entire class."

Professor Greenfeld nodded and held up a picture of this gruesome-looking creature that resembled the Loch Ness monster. "Just kidding," Mr. Greenfeld said, not cracking a smile. Then he held up another picture of a goony-looking bird. "This," he said, "is our mission."

Ms. Wilder blew the whistle sharply again and announced, "We will all reconvene here at one o'clock to report our findings and enjoy the splendid lunch I prepared."

Reluctantly, we all followed the professor and Ms. Wilder like a herd of cows. Everyone was terrified of falling into the swamp, so we stuck to the two of them like Krazy Glue.

Needless to say, no one found the yellow-bellied marsh-dweller — if there was such a creature. In fact, the only people who discovered anything were Kevin and Larry. They had stumbled into some poison ivy vines when they broke from the line, and they were itching like mad. The professor covered their arms and legs with mud to try and stop the itching, but it didn't seem to help.

By the time we returned to the bus for our picnic, I was so tired and thirsty I felt like I had swallowed a mouthful of cotton. Ms. Wilder had run ahead and spread out all these blankets and plastic containers.

"I hope she brought something decent," Jax said. "I'm dying for something to drink, like a giant soda."

"I'd even settle for water," Larry said.

Ms. Wilder stood in the middle of the blankets holding up two large jugs. "I know everyone is parched. Grab a cup from my left here and you can have your choice of a beverage. Then grab a sandwich here from the basket on my right. No need to pick through. They're all the same."

We all stumbled over and picked up our cups. I was first in line. I held up my cup to Ms. Wilder.

"Beet juice or okra juice?" she asked with an innocent little smirk.

As Jax, Chris, Matt, and I sat together on the blanket sipping some disgusting beet juice and

73

munching on pureed fig and pine nut sandwiches, we all started to feel sick.

"My stomach doesn't feel very good," Larry said, looking a little green.

"Maybe she's slowly poisoning us," Jax whispered to me. "Did you notice that Ms. Wilder, Professor Greenfeld, and the bus driver are sipping on juice boxes and eating from a different cooler?"

"I noticed," I gulped.

The only thing I knew for sure was that Ms. Wilder had gotten her revenge. But what Ms. Wilder didn't know was that we planned to get even.

Halloween was just three days away and Matt, Chris, and I made a pact on the bus ride back: Her house would definitely be one of our stops on Halloween night.

10.
The Haunting

If it wasn't for the fact that Halloween was coming, I think I would have totally lost it. Next to Christmas, Halloween was my favorite holiday of the year, and just about everybody I know starts to plan their costume at least a month in advance. No one could spoil Halloween for me. Not even Ms. Wilder.

The other thing I kept thinking was that this would be the last year we'd all get to wear costumes to school and have the Halloween parade. Dillon said that once you get to middle school they think you're too old for that stuff.

This year, I had actually spent weeks melting these plastic sticks and molding them into a custom-fitted serpent mask for my face. It was awesome.

Matt, Chris, and I decided to meet at my house, because the houses in my neighborhood were closer together. We could get more candy. We all had to be in by nine o'clock, so we figured if we started at six-thirty we'd have a good two and a half hours to hit as many houses as possible.

We mapped out our Halloween strategy the night before. From experience, we knew who gave out the apples and who handed out the good stuff. The plan was to start with my neighborhood, then do the next two over, then do Ms. Wilder's house last. She was the farthest away.

I slipped a raw egg in my pocket right before I put on my mask. Chris and Matt showed up at my house at six-thirty sharp. We were all taking old pillowcases because they held more and wouldn't break, even if they were filled to the brim.

"Ready, guys?" I asked. Chris and Matt nodded. "Ms. Wilder will never recognize us in these costumes," I laughed.

"What do you think she's giving out? Prunes?" Matt said.

Chris and I snickered. "Probably some kind of obnoxious health treat," Chris added.

The three of us charged down the street to the first good house. We weren't disappointed. The woman gave out these giant chocolate malt balls by the handful.

It took us almost an hour to do my neighborhood alone. We ran into Dillon and Weasel once. They popped out of some bushes and tried to spook us. Dillon was dressed like Freddy

Krueger and yelled, "Boo!" It was hard to tell what Weasel was supposed to be. Dillon tugged at my pillowcase and pretended he was going to steal my candy.

"Boy, we're really scared out of our wits," I said sarcastically, lifting Weasel's mask. "Knock it off," I shouted impatiently. "We knew it was you guys."

They both just laughed. "Hey," Dillon said, "you guys got quite a haul and it's only eight o'clock. We hardly have anything."

"Yeah," Weasel said, irritated. "Mostly we just get a stupid piece of candy and a dirty look. One house even turned out the lights when they saw us coming. I guess people think we're too old for this."

"So where are you guys headed next?" my brother asked. "Maybe we could join your group and we'd make out better."

"No way," I said. Matt and Chris backed me up.

Dillon gave a teasing yank at my bag, then said, "Later." They took off in the opposite direction.

We went to two more neighborhoods, and our pillowcases were so heavy, they were starting to slow us down. According to my map, we were very close to Ms. Wilder's house. I was pretty sure she was one street over on the corner. We walked over and started looking at house numbers. Matt pointed to a corner house with a

blinking skeleton and all these other cheesy deco-
rations. "That's got to be hers."

I nodded. She had a million white plastic ghosts
hanging from her trees and a couple of Styrofoam
gravestones in her yard. I recognized her car sitting in the driveway.

"Let's do it," I said. We ran up to the car. Luckily, it was unlocked. I opened the driver's-side
door and strategically placed a raw egg on the
front seat. We were all laughing through our
masks just thinking about her sitting on it and
smearing it all over. Headlights flashed from the
street, which spooked us a little, so I motioned to
Matt to quit. Quietly, I shut the car door and we
headed to her front door.

I rang the doorbell and she opened it before my
finger even left the bell.

"Trick or treat!" we yelled, holding out our pillowcases.

"My, my, my, my, what have we here?" she
screeched. "What a scary bunch you are!" Then,
to our amazement, she dropped a huge bag of
Hershey's chocolates into each of our pillowcases.
We looked at each other, stunned. "Happy Halloween!" she sang, then slammed the door.

By this time everyone's candy haul was the
biggest in our trick-or-treating history. We had a
long walk home, so we stuffed a few goodies into
our mouths while we walked. Some of the houses
started turning off their lights, and it was getting

hard to see. I looked at my glow-in-the-dark watch and was shocked to see it was almost nine.

"We'd better hurry, guys," I said. "It's later than we think."

Picking up the pace to almost a jog, we were soon almost out of breath. We'd been practically jogging for about fifteen minutes when I began to have an eerie feeling, like we were being followed. I thought I saw the dim glow of a flashlight for a second and heard footsteps in the exact rhythm of my own. Every time I turned around to check, the footsteps stopped and no one was there.

At first I didn't say anything to Matt or Chris because I didn't want them to think I was some scared wimp. But the feeling kept getting stronger. Then I heard a grunting sound, as if someone had stumbled. "Did you hear that? I think we're being followed," I whispered. They both admitted they had the same feeling.

"Maybe it's just Dillon and Weasel again," Chris said.

"I don't know," Matt said, sounding worried. "Remember? They took off in the opposite direction."

The houses were getting even farther apart. To get to the next well-lit street, we had to walk up a long, dark, winding road.

I thought I heard the footsteps again. My

palms began to sweat. I almost lost my grip on the pillowcase.

"Do you guys want to run and get there faster?" I asked.

We all took off. Someone was definitely hot on our heels, cackling like a witch. We all heard it. I looked over my shoulder and screamed bloody murder. There stood someone all in black, with two curled feet and a dark mask over its face.

"Drop your bags," this deep, throaty, horrible voice called out.

We stopped in our tracks. My hands were trembling, but I didn't let go. Matt and Chris just stood there frozen, gripping their pillowcases. I could hear Matt's teeth chattering as he said, "Don't do it. It's just some teenager in a costume."

"Run! Run!" I screamed. Matt tripped and spilled his candy. He got up stumbling and running at the same time. The person was coming after us. My heart was thumping so hard I thought it was going to fly right out of my chest.

"Faster! Run!" I screamed again. Chris's cape got caught on a tree limb. He was tearing and thrashing frantically like a hooked fish. I ran back and pulled it loose.

It was like a bad dream where you tried to run but your legs wouldn't move fast enough. Finally, we were forced to drop our pillowcases, and candy spilled over the street like broken glass.

We bolted without really knowing where we were going. "Run faster! Hurry!" I screamed.

None of us turned around until we got back to my neighborhood. When I did turn around and no one was there, we fell to the ground, our chests heaving.

I shook my head. "Do you believe this? The biggest candy haul of all time and some lunatic is probably laughing his head off and eating all our stuff."

Matt and Chris walked me back to my house, and then Chris and Matt walked home together, since they lived right next door to each other.

When I got home, I ran up to my room and screamed, "Good night." Then I shut my bedroom door and climbed under the covers. My mom tapped on the door two seconds later.

"You're home ten minutes early, honey. Now, that's a record! Did you boys have fun?"

"Yeah, it was awesome," I lied. "I'm kind of tired. Good night."

"Good night. Don't eat too much candy, now."

I had one Tootsie Roll in my pocket. I took it out and nibbled on it slowly to make it last. Then I tried to fall asleep, but I couldn't.

At ten o'clock, the doorbell rang. I was lying in bed, still shaken. I thought it was a little late for trick-or-treaters.

"I'll get it," my mother called. Then I heard her open the door and say, "What a surprise, please come in." Quickly I threw off my covers and ran to the top of the stairs so I could hear what was going on.

It took me only a second to recognize that horrible, unmistakable voice talking to my mother. Ms. Wilder!

"Hello, Mrs. Malloy, I'm Ms. Wilder, your son's substitute teacher. I was just doing my usual Halloween check-in to personally make sure that every one of my precious students made it home safe and sound."

"Well, how sweet of you, Ms. Wilder. Yes, Jeffrey is upstairs in his bed, sound asleep. Probably dreaming about all that candy he got."

I inched closer to the stairway to see if I could get a look at her, but she was blocked by our huge palm tree in the entranceway. But as she turned to leave, her feet came into view. There was no question that these were the same two curled witch's feet that had followed us that night.

11.
SANAUGI?

When Chris, Matt, and I walked into her classroom on Monday morning, Ms. Wilder was acting like her same old self, just humming away at her desk as if nothing had happened.

At this point we were hoping that maybe the egg had rolled off the driver's seat and onto the floor, still intact. I wanted to call a truce. She won. We were no match for Ms. Wilder.

At nine o'clock, while Jax was taking roll call, Ms. Wilder stood up and started writing stuff on the blackboard. That's when I saw it — smeared egg yolk dripping from the back of her dress.

Larry and some of the kids sitting in the front spotted it and were laughing hysterically. I was horrified and tried to make a shush sign with my finger to my lips, but they were unshushable.

Ms. Wilder turned around and saw Eric pointing at her dress. She ran her hand over the yolk, then wiped it on her desk.

For a second I thought she was going to freak

out, but she didn't. Instead, she smiled and said, "Ah, the sound of children's laughter. It's music to my ears." Then she blew kisses to all of us with her hands and started on the lesson.

Except for the fact that she bombarded us with "optional" homework that week, it didn't look like she was planning to retaliate. A whole three days went by, and only about a third of the kids turned in their so-called optional homework, but on Thursday Ms. Wilder threw another one of her horrible "surprise parties."

I raised my hand. "Ms. Wilder, do you think you could let us know the next time we're going to have a surprise party?"

Ms. Wilder just grinned and shook her head. "Then it wouldn't be much of a surprise, would it?"

I was sweating bullets. All I could think about the rest of the day was how to explain my bad quiz grade to my dad. The situation was almost worse than having Mr. Manlin. Who knew what the woman would pull next? I wasn't about to change my grade again — I was still feeling guilty about the last time. I decided to get my mom to sign this one. She grounded me for the rest of the week.

That Friday, I continued to do my desk inspections. They were getting pretty gross and sometimes I would have to hold my breath, but Ms. Wilder never said a word.

The following Monday Jax did the roll call and took it to the office. But something was wrong.

Kevin and Larry were both trying to get my attention, giving me these strange looks. Finally they passed a note. "RED ALERT. Willy and Milly are missing."

At recess, a few of us snuck back into the classroom to look for them. I mean, it's pretty hard to lose two giant iguanas. They were both almost a foot long, and we knew it would be hard not to see them if they escaped. At least that's what we kept telling ourselves. For the next two days we formed search parties at recess. There was no sign of them anywhere.

On the third day, Ms. Wilder came into the classroom with a tray of little plastic cups and wooden spoons. She asked one of the kids to pass them out.

Matt raised his hand. "Ms. Wilder, what is this stuff?" he asked, making a face.

"It's avocado ice mixed with a few natural ingredients," she said. "I made it especially for all of you. I will take personal offense if you won't at least try it." Well, nobody wanted to endure her "personal offense," so we all reluctantly took a small taste.

To my surprise, it was delicious. A lot of the

kids even finished it and asked for more. But Ms. Wilder said only one to a customer. There wasn't enough for everyone to have seconds. When we finished she asked Larry to walk around with a little wastebasket and collect the cups and spoons.

Then Jax raised her hand and said, "Ms. Wilder, could you tell us how you made it?"

"I'd be happy to," she said, smiling. "It's one part avocado, a pinch of fruit juice, a touch of honey, and a special secret ingredient. I call it 'Sanaugi dessert.'" She wrote SANAUGI in big letters across the blackboard.

Then this real smart kid raised his hand. He was also dyslexic and read a lot of things backward. "Ms. Wilder, isn't Sanaugi 'iguanas' spelled backward?"

Ms. Wilder started rubbing her stomach in circles and rolled her eyes up in their sockets.

We all started laughing. Ms. Wilder really did have a sense of humor after all. We laughed and we laughed.

Then two more days went by and there was still no sign of Willy and Milly. We all stopped laughing.

12.
The Confrontation

I hardly slept the night we found out that we'd eaten Milly and Willy. I decided it was time to take the matter into my own hands.

I called for a strategy meeting. After school the following Monday, Matt, Chris, and I took the bus to my house. We even invited Jax and Becca to come.

We all gathered in my tree house to make a plan.

"I think we should go to the principal," Jax said firmly. "The woman needs some serious help."

Chris shook his head. "I don't know about talking to Mr. Carson. We'd have to tell him everything. And then what? We'd all probably get expelled when he finds out what we were doing in the classroom."

"He's right," Jax agreed. "We weren't exactly perfect little students before Ms. Wilder came."

"What if we told her we knew she made us eat Milly and Willy and that we would expose her evil doings if she didn't stop," Becca suggested.

"What if that made her angrier?" Chris said. "Who knows, we could be eating one of our classmates by the end of the week. She's too unpredictable. I wouldn't put anything past her."

"Me neither," Matt agreed. "For our own safety, I think we should lay low for a while. You know, just be on our best behavior. Don't pull any more pranks or things on her."

"Well, I've had it," I said. "I'm going to confront her face-to-face. I'll do the talking." I looked Matt in the eye. "I just want you and Chris to be there and back me up when I tell her we're going to the principal if she doesn't resign."

"It's a deal," Matt said.

"Deal," Chris said.

"What if she does resign?" Becca asked. "Who knows what kind of a substitute we'd get next?"

"Becca," I said, "who could possibly be worse than Ms. Wilder? She makes Godzilla look like a pussycat, and that's on a good day."

Everyone thought that was pretty funny.

"Okay, then," I said. "Tomorrow we do it. Lunchtime."

We all put our hands together and made a pact.

The next morning I was a nervous wreck, but I was determined to do it. Enough was enough. At about eleven-thirty that morning everyone was putting their books away, about to go to lunch.

Chris, Matt, and I stalled, pretending to be looking for something in our cubbies.

I took a long, deep breath and said, "Let's go, guys," out of the corner of my mouth. I led the way, and Matt and Chris kind of trailed behind. We stood in front of Ms. Wilder's desk. I cleared my throat and she looked up.

"Yes?" she said, raising her eyebrows. "What is it?"

I was so scared my knees were shaking. My mouth went dry. I cleared my throat again. "Ms. Wilder, there's something I need to ask you," I said, my voice cracking.

She smiled sweetly. "Ask away, Jeffrey."

"Well, ever since you've been our substitute teacher, we have all noticed that a lot of strange things have been happening." I nudged Matt and Chris with my elbow to back me up with at least a "Yeah" or something, but they both acted like they didn't own a voice.

Ms. Wilder's eyes grew bigger by the minute, but she was still smiling. She looked me right in the eye. "I'm afraid I don't know what you're talking about, Jeffrey. I am just doing my job and hoping that some of the things I teach you kids stick in those brains of yours."

I could see I was getting nowhere fast. I felt myself getting madder, which must have made me braver. "I know you know what I'm talking about. You've been trying to trick us, making us think we were going to Hershey Park and all."

"And all?"

I gulped so loud it echoed throughout the classroom. "We know that was you who was following us around on Halloween trying to scare us."

Her eyes widened so much, they looked like they would pop right out of her head, but she said nothing.

I was on a roll. "You fed us those iguanas, didn't you?"

"What on earth are you talking about?"

"The iguanas that were living in Eric's and Chris's desks. Willy and Milly," I said, my voice shaking.

"Did you say Milly?" she screamed. "Milly?" Then her face started turning purple and her eyes looked like they were going to jump from her head. "My name is Ms. Mildred Wilder. Not Milly Wilder. Not Mrs. Mildred Wilder. It's Ms. Mildred Wilder!"

My heart fell to my feet. Matt and Chris started to back out of the room.

"Not so fast," she screamed at them. "Yes! Yes! You're absolutely right. I've had enough of your pranks and antics," she snarled.

Frantically rooting through her desk, she then pulled out three pieces of paper. She shoved them at me. "Someone's been a naughty boy," she said, now calmer. I looked at the papers she was dangling in front of our noses. It was the test that we had all changed our grades on.

I was speechless. She shook her finger at each of us. "Naughty. Naughty. Naughty."

We all just looked at each other. We were at her mercy. She knew she had us by our naughty little necks.

I shuddered to think what she had planned for us next.

13.
The Trip to
New York City

The following morning, my worst nightmare came true. Ms. Wilder passed out permission slips for a field trip to New York City. As a special surprise, she was taking our class to see the Statue of Liberty the very next day.

Everyone knows that people disappear in New York all the time. I didn't want to be one of them.

"This trip was a very last-minute opportunity," Ms. Wilder said as she finished passing out the slips. "It just so happens that a friend of mine had a trip cancellation and a bus has been made available. It's going to be such fun. We're even going to get to take a ferry ride over to Ellis Island. Hope everyone knows how to swim," she said, half grinning.

I know I wasn't the only one who was shaking in my boots. Even Larry got a sick look on his face and mouthed the words "no way" to me. I saved about six seats at the lunch table so we could put our heads together.

"I'm going to be sick tomorrow," Matt said, putting his hand to his forehead like he already had a temperature brewing.

"I was going to be sick, too," I said. Then Chris and everyone else started saying the same thing. "We can't all be sick," I said. "Ms. Wilder will just cancel the trip and reschedule it."

"Well, do you have any other bright ideas?" Jax asked, looking at me.

"Let me think," I said, sipping my milk, trying to stall. "I've got it! We could each write notes on the permission slips saying something like, 'New York is too far, please put so and so in the library for the day.' She won't get the permission slips until right before we're ready to leave, so she won't have time to cancel the trip."

"Well, what about the rest of the class? What if she plans to take them up to the Statue of Liberty and do something to them?"

I shook my head. "Nah, we're the ones she really wants to get. If we're not there, maybe she won't pull anything." Everyone was in full agreement with the plan.

The next morning, about seven of us had notes explaining why we couldn't go. To everyone's horror, Ms. Wilder pulled a fast one.

We weren't in our seats two minutes when she said that the permission slips wouldn't be necessary. She had personally contacted each parent that very morning and gotten verbal permission because the trip was so last-minute.

"We're goners," Larry said as we lined up to get on the bus.

"Oh, no," Jax panicked, "look who's driving the bus."

We looked over at the driver's seat. It was the maniac from the trip to Hershey. He had a wild, faraway look in his eyes.

We were all pretty quiet on the trip up. Ms. Wilder must have asked us all a thousand times if everyone knew how to swim.

"She's planning to get us on the ferry," I said to Matt and Chris.

"Let's stick close together. Don't go anywhere near the edge of the boat," Chris said.

"Don't worry," I replied. Matt just got really quiet.

Finally, the bus pulled up to the ferry and we lined up and climbed aboard. As soon as the ride began, everyone was straining to see the Statue of Liberty across the harbor. At first, we didn't notice Larry was missing, but I turned to say something to him and he wasn't anywhere to be seen. I nudged Matt and Jax and Chris, and we all started looking around. But there was no sign of Larry.

"Excuse me, Ms. Wilder, do you know where Larry is?" I called out, but she didn't answer.

That's when we realized she was missing, too.

Next came a bloodcurdling scream and the captain shouted, "Man overboard! Throw down a life raft!" Whistles were blowing and everyone was screaming their heads off. We all heard a splash and ran to the side of the ferry to see Larry screaming and flailing his arms, then being pulled from the water.

Luckily he was okay, just shaken up. One of the crew members gave him some dry clothes and yelled at him for climbing past a DANGER: NO TRESPASSING sign that was posted.

Suddenly Ms. Wilder reappeared and acted shocked about the whole incident. Larry took a seat between Jax and me and shivered and shook all the way to Ellis Island.

"What happened?" we whispered. "Did you slip?" Larry shook his head, then said the three words we dreaded hearing from his quivering lips: "She pushed me."

Blood drained from our faces, and the rest of us joined him in shivering the rest of the way.

When we got to the Statue of Liberty, we all started to climb the stairs to get to the first landing, at the foot of the statue.

Upon reaching the landing, Ms. Wilder blew her whistle and yelled, "HALT! Okay, we're now at the foot of the statue. To get to the crown, we have to go up a spiral staircase. However, only eight people at a time can be inside the crown. The rest of us will stand on the staircase until each group gets their turn to look out the windows and have a chance to view the harbor."

Matt, Chris, Jax, and I exchanged anxious looks. Jax was right. She didn't want any witnesses. She broke us into groups. She put me, Matt, Chris, Larry, Kevin, Jax, and Becca in one group. The rest of the class was divided into two other groups. We were sure this was no coincidence. I started to feel sick. I raised my hand.

"Yes?" Ms. Wilder asked with a sinister smile.

"Would it be okay if I just waited here? See, I've had a fear of heights since I was little."

Ms. Wilder's smile grew wider. "Well, Jeffrey, what a wonderful opportunity this will be for you to work through your fears." She blew the whistle again. "First group, walk up." She waited with our group.

When Ms. Wilder wasn't looking, Matt pulled out a rope he had hidden in his jacket. He tied the rope around his waist, then passed the end to me. I started to wrap it around me, but Ms. Wilder caught us and, without saying a word, yanked it out of my hands.

The second group went into the crown, and soon we were next. "Come along," she sang.

When we got to the top, we all cautiously walked around inside the crown and looked at everything. We stuck to each other like glue. So far, everything was going pretty normally. "Gee," I whispered to Matt, "I guess we were all just being paranoid for nothing. I think we're home free."

"We're alive!" Matt shouted.

Of course, we still had to make it back down. Anything could happen. But three hundred and fifty-four exhausting steps later, we reached the lobby alive. The muscles in my legs were cramping. "Water, water," some of the kids were calling out, holding their parched throats. Ms. Wilder was waiting for us with this stupid little grin.

"Okay, line up. Time for a head count," she called out. "Bet some of you are rather thirsty. Now, we've got just enough time to have a little refreshment. The bus leaves promptly at three, so let's not dilly-dally," she said, leading the way to the ferry.

When we got off the ferry, Ms. Wilder led us to this place called *Jerry's Juice Castle*. There was a giant blender in the window and a sign that read TODAY'S SPECIAL, RIND-OSAURUS.

"No way I'm drinking any more beet juice or whatever it is she has in mind," Matt said. Chris pointed to a hot dog cart selling sodas right next to us. When she wasn't looking, we hung back a little and bought two grape sodas to split.

After we paid the vendor, I yelled, "C'mon,

guys, we'd better catch up." I could only guess the torture we would be put through if we got her angry. I mean, she probably had some relative that ran a dungeon or something. We made it onto the bus just in time.

14.
Welcome Back,
Mr. Manlin

When we finally returned from New York City, Ms. Wilder got off the bus with us, then just disappeared into thin air. Even our principal couldn't explain it. But secretly, a few of us knew the truth.

She was out there somewhere, waiting. Probably, when we least expect it, she'll resurface. We'll hear that horrible, screechy voice singing, "I'm back!" I only hope I'm in middle school by the time it happens.

Luckily for all of us, Ms. Wilder was the last substitute teacher we had for the year. I never thought I'd say it, but I couldn't wait to have Mr. Manlin back.

As it turned out, Larry's uncle Butch never did have a fight with Mr. Manlin. In fact, Uncle Butch was an ex-Marine and he and Mr. Manlin got along so well the day they met, they decided to take a fishing trip together. They also decided that Larry was in desperate need of discipline,

101

and later started him on this regimen that made the army look like kindergarten. Larry came clean and finally admitted to everyone that Ms. Wilder didn't really push him off the ferry — he was in a place he shouldn't have been and slipped.

Anyway, Mr. Manlin came back permanently the Monday after our New York trip. Everybody was pretty nervous that morning, even the Boyez twins. Mr. Carson came in first thing to make sure we were all under control without a teacher in the room. He had nothing to worry about. We were all being good as gold.

About five minutes later, Mr. Manlin came walking into the room. He looked around, surveying the class. "Well," he said, "I see everyone has managed to survive without me."

A few people giggled. Then everybody stood up and clapped.

Mr. Manlin gave us one of his stern looks. "Before we start our lesson, I have something you might be interested in seeing." We were all holding our breath, hoping we weren't in trouble for our past actions.

Mr. Manlin left the room for a few minutes, then came back in with none other than Willy and Milly. They had grown so big, he had them on leashes.

"I found them in the teacher's lounge with a little note attached for Class 512. I suppose it must have some importance to a few of you." He proceeded to read the note:

> "*Substitute teachers*
> *deserve a lot*
> *of slack.*
> *Be good to them,*
> *my children.*
> *Or I'll be back.*"

He smiled, but said nothing more about it. "Now, if you'll open your history books to page 168, we can begin."

Believe me when I say there wasn't one person who didn't race to page 168. Even Larry.

APPLE® PAPERBACKS

Pick an Apple and Polish Off Some Great Reading!

BEST-SELLING APPLE TITLES

❏ MT43944-8	**Afternoon of the Elves**	Janet Taylor Lisle	**$2.99**
❏ MT41624-3	**The Captive**	Joyce Hansen	**$3.50**
❏ MT43266-4	**Circle of Gold**	Candy Dawson Boyd	**$3.50**
❏ MT44064-0	**Class President**	Johanna Hurwitz	**$3.50**
❏ MT45436-6	**Cousins**	Virginia Hamilton	**$3.50**
❏ MT43130-7	**The Forgotten Door**	Alexander Key	**$2.95**
❏ MT44569-3	**Freedom Crossing**	Margaret Goff Clark	**$3.50**
❏ MT42858-6	**Hot and Cold Summer**	Johanna Hurwitz	**$3.50**
❏ MT25514-2	**The House on Cherry Street 2: The Horror**		
	Rodman Philbrick and Lynn Harnett		**$3.50**
❏ MT41708-8	**The Secret of NIMH**	Robert C. O'Brien	**$3.99**
❏ MT42882-9	**Sixth Grade Sleepover**	Eve Bunting	**$3.50**
❏ MT42537-4	**Snow Treasure**	Marie McSwigan	**$3.50**
❏ MT42378-9	**Thank You, Jackie Robinson**	Barbara Cohen	**$3.99**

Available wherever you buy books, or use this order form

Scholastic Inc., P.O. Box 7502, 2931 East McCarty Street, Jefferson City, MO 65102

Please send me the books I have checked above. I am enclosing $_____ (please add $2.00 to cover shipping and handling). Send check or money order—no cash or C.O.D.s please.

Name_____Birthdate_____

Address_____

City_____State/Zip_____

Please allow four to six weeks for delivery. Offer good in U.S. only. Sorry mail orders are not available to residents of Canada. Prices subject to change.   APP596